Delusional

Why Visioners See The Path Where Others Don't

An inspiring philosophical fairytale for grown-ups about partnering with your fears on a journey from "not made to be" to "destined to become"

Dreamer: "I have done everything I could"

Universe: "I know, now it's my turn…"

By Iryana

Cover Art By: Slobodan "Srdjan" Vukovic

Illustrations By: Victoria Trum

Published by Screw Leadership Corp

ISBN: 979-8-9884631-7-7

A Tribute to Ukraine

Iconic leadership can come from the most unexpected places.

Ukraine is my homeland, the country where I was born and raised until the age of 19. It remains a home for much of my family and friends.

I see a lot of subtle parallels between the story in this book and the story of leadership and resilience that unfolded in Ukraine in light of the brutal and devastating Russian invasion.

I am filled with pride for the way Ukraine is standing up in the face of the monster, and the way the Ukrainian people all over the world instantly united to defend their home and fascinate the world with their unbreakable faith and unshakeable resilience.

In the face of beastly challenges that were "guaranteed" to break it to pieces, Ukraine "came together" with all it had, and the world followed and came together for Ukraine, for Freedom, for Justice.

I want to thank every single soul who helped, prayed for Ukraine and its people and who stands up for what is right despite the hefty price tag.

Delusional

I was giving the name of this book a lot of thought and have gone through dozens of options. I asked myself: "What unites all visionaries, all innovators, all rebels?" At first, I just called it a vision or a voice of their soul. Actually, you will see that in this story, the word "vision" is at the front and center, because that's what drives the main character to keep hoping, keep dreaming, and...to start acting.

But you know what is another common denominator of remarkable people? It is *trust* in this voice that tells them: "Go. The path will appear when you've made it far enough. You will know what to do."

Over the years I have learned about hundreds of success stories of all the people, innovations, and businesses, that weren't "supposed" to succeed, if not for some *coincidence*. I realized that there is an elevated level of belief that visioners have: they believe that *the right things will coincide at the right time.*

This knowledge-like faith is a catalyst that turns uncertainty into action for those who have it. When we ask for a lucky break in life, it is this knowledge-like faith that defines what we do with that "break" once we get it. It defines whether we turn it into a break-down or a break-through.

This story is about that. The main character, the little screw named Martin, has been dreaming of becoming a part of a watch his entire life. He always thought it would take a human to accomplish his dream until he understood that a human may or may not see him as a good fit. That was the "break" he had been asking for, and he could either keep hoping or act on his belief and do everything in his power to accomplish the unthinkable: to build a watch with the sole efforts of the watch parts that didn't even know if they had it in them.

Martin faces a lot of obstacles in his journey. One of those obstacles would almost certainly make him give up on his dream, if only he knew about it in advance. Instead, his blind faith guided him just far enough that he could watch the universe in action. A path appeared in the most unexpected way. A magic coincidence that represents what many visioners experienced on the brink of "all is lost..."

A lot of people who follow their voice can attest to the moment when it seems that you cry out to the universe: "I have done everything I could," and the Universe responds: " I know. Now it's my turn…"

So, why "delusional?" Because knowledge-like faith is seeing the path where it *will* appear, just at the end of your capacity, and *knowing* it will be there when you arrive.

Preface

The only thing people love more than telling you who you *are*, is telling you who you *are not* and what you *won't* accomplish.

This short story invites you to dare to challenge, dare to question, dare to break down the limiting gates of what or who *someone says* you are. Let's break down the shackles of the fear-driven "logic" that dictates that you have to have all the answers before setting out on a path. After all, the path may take you someplace you didn't know existed.

You won't know who you *could become* if you don't challenge everything you *are* supposedly *not.* You will not know where you *could* go if you do not challenge the boundaries of someone else's maps.

What would happen if you didn't come with a "label…"?

Chapter 1- The Dream

"Shhhh, guys, be quiet, I think we have a visitor!" Martin jumped out of the old drawer to get further away from the never-ending chatter and hear what was going on.

"Do you see this? Did someone finally come to buy the old watch store?" A spark of hope illuminated Martin's already optimistic face. He froze, daydreaming about the possibilities lying ahead if the store were to have a new owner.

The once lively and charmingly messy watch repair store had been sitting empty for quite some time. It had been waiting for the new owner ever since Larry, the jolly old owner, fell ill and was forced by his family to retire.

Ah… the good old days, Martin reminisced to himself. *Larry always treated every little watch part with respect. Look at Jose, an old beat-up and discolored crystal — anybody would just toss him straight into the garbage! But not Larry! He always said: 'I bet this guy has a story to tell,' and he would put each one of them, old-timer used parts, into our 'storyteller' drawer. Well, that's what we like to call it anyway. Of course, the drawer with new parts had another name for us— 'the pity basket,' but that's just their opinion. Being small and replaceable, I've had plenty of offers of offense in my lifetime, but I've always refused them. To me, it's a no-brainer. When someone offers you an opinion that makes you feel bad, just let them keep it and stick with your own. It is just one point of view, everyone is entitled to their own.* Martin got carried away by his thoughts like usual.

"Oh stop it, you little dreamy thing," Julie interrupted Martin's fantasies. "You're just a little screw, and you'll be lucky if the new owner will even keep you in the little 'pity basket,' forget about ever making it into a watch! Who uses old parts, especially the..."

Julie stopped, realizing how bad this was about to sound. "Well… you know what I mean …no offense." She toned down, hoping that she hadn't crossed the line between bringing Martin down to earth and making him feel like complete useless crap.

"Noooone taaaaken!" Martin cheerfully replied with a surprising southern accent. "I don't need to *think*. I *feel* that my destiny has something very special in store for me."

"Oh, Martin…" said Julie with pity in her voice. Though not that old, everything he had been through in his lifetime had left its mark, and he was already showing some rust. *Why couldn't he just enjoy early retirement and give up his unrealistic hopes,* she thought to herself.

Among the new shiny parts, Julie was the most… humble…Well, if that word can be applied to any of them. The fact that she wasn't too full of herself was actually a little surprising. Besides being new, she was also one of the main characters. She was the hands that gracefully moved around the dial with her pretty little arrows showing the time.

The doorbell, who was deep asleep due to the lack of visitors for what had seemed like ages, was startled by his own "ding." The front door finally opened.

Martin was all ears."Well, Mister…" started Tony, the old realtor friend of Larry's.

"Just Evan," said a slim man with big radiant eyes and a happy facial expression, whose voice sounded too mature for his youthful appearance.

"As I told you, Mister Evan, the shop has been closed for a while, so it needs some work to bring it back to its glory days," continued Tony.

"Didn't you say the old guy used to design watches from spare parts?" asked Evan.

"Oh, yes… the old man had this funny idea that someone would like the .." started Tony, only to be quickly interrupted by Evan.

"That's exactly my plan for this place - I want it to be my creative lab! I think the old man was onto something," Evan interrupted him. "But, if I were to buy the store, I'd want to include the seller's signature watch pieces in the deal, if I find them to my taste."

"Oh.." exhaled Tony with noticeable disappointment, "I don't know if the old man would agree to that… Even if he did, I don't know if you will find his creations to your taste. In all honesty, that part of the business has earned old Larry nothing but ridicule," said Tony. Tony seemed to have assumed this deal would never happen, so without further ado, he started making his way to the door and out of the shop, before Evan even got a chance to take a close enough look around.

Evan glanced around the store, stopping his gaze at the worktable, staring at it, almost as if he was trying to catch the glimpse of the past and see the old man working on his masterpieces. *I have a good feeling about this one,* he thought to himself.

"Tell you what," said Evan, rushing after Tony's heavy figure. "Why don't you talk to the old man and see if he will agree to meet with me and show me his pieces. I think we can reach an agreement."

Tony rolled his eyes and said somewhat dismissively: "You got it kiddo, I'll give you a buzz after I talk to him."

Martin was so excited that he lost his grip and fell back inside the drawer.

"Guys! Did you hear this? It's our time to shine!" Martin was radiating excitement.

"What are you talking about?" asked Jose, the old, discolored crystal, in his heavy Mexican accent.

"This guy, Evan, he is *it!* He is the one we have been waiting for! He will buy the shop and continue building signature pieces, and we will finally become a part of the watch that the old man envisioned for us!"

"Oh, this again," said Frederique, the pompous French wristband. "The pity basket WAS the masterpiece model." He made a frame with his fingers. "'The Graveyard'!" He continued laughing, still holding the frame of his fingers up to Martin's face.

"Oh Martin," said Mrs. Dila, the dial, pushing arrogant Frederique out of the way. "Don't take it to heart, sweetheart, but don't you think there is a reason the old man never created the watch with all of us? I mean, look at us, my color is faded, I have a green hue for crying out loud! Jose, nice guy, but the discoloration on the crystal... his story is finished. Sorry Jose," she said as she turned to him.

"Oh, don't worry Señorita, I know my song is sung, I have no aspirations. Estoy contento," replied Jose.

"Besides," continued Mrs. Dila, "we don't have the back cover, neither in our drawer nor amongst those 'newbies.' Old Larry used the last one for a repair job he did not long before retiring. Our path is over, my friend, let's face it and accept our part with dignity."

"Absolutely not!" Martin wouldn't give up "I have a VISION, I know that together we will make one unique watch!"

Frederique couldn't help but make his usual sarcastic remark: "Well, for that to come true, that new kid on the block has to be delusional just like you. Maybe you can transfer your 'vision' to him while he sleeps!" he said almost bending to the floor from laughter.

"You know what?" Martin exclaimed unphased by the cruel joke, "That is exactly what I am going to do!"

"Oh, boy," whispered Julie to Mrs. Dila with great concern, "I think Martin may have finally lost it…"

"Okay, okay, why are you all staring at me like I turned into a giraffe? I'm not a lunatic and I know I cannot transfer my vision to Evan when he is asleep," said Martin in an unusually calm voice, as if he was trying to emphasize just how sane and adequate he was. This tone did not last however, as excitement took over him again and he exclaimed: "But we can *build* that same watch that we were all meant for, and I am sure Evan will love it!"

For a few minutes, Martin's face froze in an expression of excitement, hopefulness, and anticipation of support, when suddenly notes of encouraging voice broke the silence: "What a great idea, Martin!" That, unfortunately, was from Frederique. "That way you can all go down together in a …how should I put it…since you couldn't really call that a watch…" He was demonstratively tapping on his chin and directing his squinting eyes to the ceiling as if seriously thinking about something. "Oh, I know! 'Used part convention!'" He finished smugly, almost bursting from the pride of his wit.

Parts started slowly walking away, having not said anything about the idea to Martin's face, but discussing behind his back just how crazy he and his plans were. "We are just small parts. We are not supposed to *make* watches. We've never done it," some said. "What is he thinking, that poor fool, that we can be anything? We can just wish to become a watch and 'boom,' it's done?!" said others. "And how would we even know what to do? That's just ridiculous, we have no master to put us together," the rest murmured their responses.

Martin knew he was right. The image in his mind was so clear - the watch he and his shelf-mates could make was brilliant! Sure, he may not know everything about the mechanisms of the watch and would need some help, but he was sure that together as a team, they would fill in the blanks. After all, when the watch was finished and assembled, each part would know all of his neighbors and what their jobs were. He knew he had to psych himself up and then convince every one of those parts to buy into his vision.

What if something went wrong, he thought. *What if someone, just one part, decided to not cooperate? That would be the end of the story.* Doubts started casting a shadow on his plan and worrisome thoughts kept coming: *Some parts had no ambition at all, and they may very well be happy with their retirement. Others had more spark than they showed.*

Old Jose, for example, used to belong to a Marine General. He picked up quite a few traits from the military. While he was rather quiet and unassuming, one look at him would be enough to know how tough he was. His service as a crystal was no longer possible, due to the extensive fogging that clouded the dial underneath. Despite his beat-up looks though, it was undeniable that he was stronger and more capable than most crystals half his age.

Realizing that, as always, he got carried away by his thoughts, Martin brought himself back to reality:
Okay, I need to start with a plan. First: design a mechanism. Scratch that. First: learn what one needs to know to design a mechanism.

Ah…who am I kidding? I don't have the time to learn, especially since I do not know what is it that I do not know! How do you learn that?

> **I do not know what is it that I do not know! How do you learn that?**

No, this is definitely a bad plan. What if everybody is right, and this is just a bad idea altogether?

But I have a vision! I know deep down this is what I was meant for, all I need is for others to understand me…

The idea dawned on him so suddenly that he stumbled back a step.

Yes! That's right! I need others to understand me. So let's start there. I only need two things: a "who," the team… and a "why," the reason why we all need to do this.

Well, I know who the teammates are, let's focus on why. If only I could make them believe that my vision is true and that they will all be happy if we follow through with my plan! I think I saw a book on hypnosis on the old man's table…

He continued scheming to himself, almost jumping from the jolts of positive energy he felt. He kept going back to the vision of the unique masterpiece that he and his friends were destined to be a part of. Who knows, maybe they would get to travel the world or attend a university…speculations of who will wear the watch were teasing his imagination with images of possibilities.

Chapter 2 – Leadership

Martin approached everyone, but nobody would listen to him. He heard endless excuses addressing every possible doubt, from whether they had enough parts, not only for the looks of the watch but for the mechanism behind it, to the fact that none of them had the expertise necessary to design and build a watch! Martin was devastated, and thoughts that he was just a little screw, one that nobody even saw, started coming down on him.

Of course, they don't believe in me, he thought. *I am not even a major player, I'm just a little screw, and not even one with a fancy Swiss pedigree…how can I lead them? And I don't want to lead anyone, I just want to be a part of the team that works like…well…like clockwork!* That little analogy made him chuckle, though that was but a brief distraction from his despair.

"Señor Martin…" he heard a mellow voice with an unmistakable Mexican accent belonging to Jose.

"The best leaders are not the ones that beat themselves in the chest and have all the answers."

"Who are the best leaders then, Jose?" Martin lifted his sad gaze to look the Marine in the eye.

"The best leaders are those who make the best teammates. They are the best team players, attributing successes to the team and faults to themself. The best leaders know how to cheer up a teammate when they need it, they know what everybody's strengths and weaknesses are. They make sure every player is in the best possible place to shine.

"Some will be in a position to command a group of people, and they call themselves leaders, but a true leader is someone who is at the very center of the *culture*, not the *attention*. Someone who creates a ripple effect from within, whose passion radiates through the teammates they inspire, and whose strength emanates from personal humility."

"What does humility have to do with anything?!" Martin asked

"Well, my friend, humility is freedom…"

"Freedom?!" Martin interrupted him. "What is so freeing about being a humble pushover? Look at me – I am humble, but I wouldn't say that I feel free. I feel…lonely. "

"Freedom and loneliness - they are the two sides of the same coin. All you need to do is flip it."

"But how do I flip it?" – Martin asked with a puzzled look on his face

"Loneliness exists for a reason – it provides the space to think deeply and get to the core of what is important to you. It takes a lot of courage to not run away from loneliness. If you embrace it, you will come to great strength that will become contagious enough for others to follow you. Then you will discover freedom."

Martin was listening intently, realizing that Jose's words were resonating with him on some level. He always felt that he had a special destiny. Deep down he also knew that he needed to step up to the challenge and earn his teammates' support. His thoughts were interrupted once again by Jose:

"And who said anything about being a pushover? Do you know how many high-ranking officers I have seen who bolster their achievements and brag about their influence? The loud ones always ended up proving themselves to be slaves to their self-image and self-interest. Those were never impactful leaders, as all they cared about was shining the spotlight on themselves.

"I will give you contrasts of two leaders and you tell me which one you'd follow if you had a choice," continued Jose.

"Officer A takes credit for everything done by the team and prides himself on the excellent results he's achieved as a superior officer. Officer B gives credit to everybody who actually deserves it and distinguishes team players for their talents.

"When there are shortcomings, Officer A assigns blame to one of the team players and reprimands him. Officer B, in contrast, wants to understand what systems he implemented that didn't work correctly, resulting in an undesired event. He wants to address the problem by optimizing everybody's role and fixing ineffective systems and guidelines.

"Which one would you choose?" finally asked Jose

"I would choose Officer B," admitted Martin. "He sounds like a much nicer fella and I wouldn't be afraid of him."

"That is because he wears humility with pride. He receives satisfaction from seeing his vision..." Jose winked, "come to life, and *enjoys sharing that joy with all those who helped make it happen.* Every little screw that holds the parts together.

"Officer A is an arrogant 'leader,' who is shackled by dependence on the opinions and approval of others. A close enough look at him will reveal that he lives in terror caused by the instability of his sense of self-worth. Such people are at war with the world to prove that they are worthy.

"When one cares for their image above all, they will never be a good team player, let alone a leader. The best leaders are made of the best team players. Do you see my point now?" asked Jose with a subtle smile.

"I never thought of it that way, but I guess I do see it now…" Martin replied.

"Well, I know of one very good team player with a vision, but, before he can make others believe in him, he has to throw away everything that holds him back."

"But how?" Martin asked, still full of doubting thoughts.

"These youngsters…" Jose shook his head slowly, suppressing any frustration. "What did I just say about humility?"

"Well, that a good leader thinks about the good of the team, not of himself" Martin was hoping that if he shows he is a good and attentive student, Jose will take him out of his misery and just give him a straight answer.

"Yes…and what have you been doing sitting here all sad?" Jose was adamant about leading Martin to find answers on his own.

"Thinking that I am not…"

"Exactamente!" Jose exclaimed, happy that Martin bit the bait, "You were thinking about YOU!"

"But I wasn't being arrogant or anything," Martin started apologetically, "I just…"

"No, no, no, stop right there! One sentence and two 'I's already! It's not about YOU! It doesn't matter whether you attach a positive or negative to the 'I', it is still the same 'I'!

"But then how am I…oops…how is 'someone' supposed to lead, if they are not even sure whether they are good enough?" Martin was totally confused

"They are not supposed to make it about themselves at all. A leader serves a purpose. All he needs to focus on is the purpose he is serving. If he focuses on that, he cannot be 'not good enough.'

"Or do you think anyone can do better than *their own* best?" Jose said looking Martin in the eye as if he was trying to plant this idea straight into his soul.

"Of course not," Martin answered without even thinking

"Can someone be not good enough to do *their* best?" Jose asked a follow-up question.

"I guess not unless they are not motivated" – Martin was starting to understand where Jose was going with it.

"That's right, lack of motivation will prevent someone from doing their best. That is why life gave you the space where you feel lonely. As we discussed, this is the space where you will find out what really matters to you and what isn't worth the trouble."

"You know, I do feel that if we all just did our best, it would be enough. I feel motivated, but I just don't know how to motivate others." Martin admitted.

"That is because you think that to motivate others, you need to 'sell' them something. You have to understand that you will never overpower anyone. Tricking others only goes so far. However, if you can find the common need that everybody in the team has, you will be able to spark a light in each of their hearts and their motivation will follow."

Martin was visibly saddened by being brought to the realization that there seems to be a lot of work involved in *getting* others on board.

"It is always easy to fall back on an excuse, amigo. This is where your loyalty to the cause is tested. You may have been endowed with a leadership task, but only when you find answers on your own, will the leader in you be born." Jose got up from his seat and started walking away, leaving Martin deeply immersed in a thought process that was making him feel somewhere between inspired and terrified.

Chapter 3 – The Dreamer

This was the time for deep inner reflection. Martin realized that nobody believed in his 'vision,' because it was nothing but an empty word.

The problem he faced was that when he was trying to define his goal, it boiled down to "making a watch" from parts that were neither excited about such perspective, nor, frankly speaking, in the best shape for the task.

Martin himself wasn't excited about making a watch per se. It dawned on him that the *goal* had little to do with the *purpose*. The goal was just a means to an end.

The purpose was something completely different. Martin started thinking back, trying to determine how long he has been dreaming about being a part of a watch. He always believed himself to be a *visionary*, not just a *dreamer*, hopeful and inspiring, **not** unrealistic and delusional. But was it actually so?

Well, did he know the difference between a visionary and a dreamer? Both dream and both can inspire others and yet there is a gap between them. On one side he would find accomplishment and fulfillment while the other side held failure and empty clouds of dreams once dreamt.

Appears then, that all visionaries start as dreamers. The difference is obviously in follow-through. One will take the dream and turn it into reality and the other will take it and keep it, maybe share it with others.

This was the very crossroad on which Martin now found himself. Having been gifted with a vivid imagination, just watching his dream unfold in his mind gave him immense pleasure. Nothing threatened this perfect picture in a dream. Was that what he was afraid of? Losing his dream? After all, if he focused only on all things that would make its fulfillment impossible, he would no longer be able to keep his fairytale. That alternate reality that has always been there for him, practically on demand, his whole life. Was he afraid to wake up to the "real life" that everyone has been telling him about? But how about all the stories he had heard of those who made the impossible possible? Does impossibility then even exist? Who first challenged it? A lunatic or a visionary?

This turning point was very uncomfortable for Martin because he could no longer remain whom he *thought* himself to be. There was no longer an option to keep dreaming because this was the final call. He was not delusional. A drawer full of old parts would surely be quickly discarded by anyone who takes over the store, and after that, his dream would be nothing but a sad story of what could have been.

And maybe this retrospective alternative will still give him some pleasure, knowing that it was a matter of *chance* and that the cards were just not in his favor.

But now that he is aware of the imminent change, he actually has the opportunity to do something about it and throw himself and all his effort into the universe. Giving himself to the hope that destiny will catch him in her warm embrace, before his dreams shattered falling into a bottomless pit, only to echo in his mind until rust slowly eats away his entire little body.

No, he can no longer be a dreamer, he must face it, and either be a visionary or a failure.

Martin realized that there are two possible ways to relate to one's desires, plans, or dreams: either be **inspired by them** or be **imprisoned by them**. It dawned on him that he had been paralyzed by his dream so far, why else hasn't he been able to move forward?

There are two possible ways to relate to one's desires, plans, or dreams: either be <u>inspired by them</u> or be <u>imprisoned by them</u>.

His face was illuminated with a subtle feeling of freedom and contentment as he realized that a visionary is not someone who makes his vision come true. It is someone who, inspired by their vision, takes just one step into the *unknown*. The sense of false security from daydreaming was finally shed, and, after a brief moment of terror where he realized there was a possibility of failure, came the moment of freedom.

He found his purpose. No, it wasn't about making a watch. It was about freeing himself and others from the prison of the mind. They all felt like their destiny was in someone else's hands.

Martin knew that it was too much to expect that someone will have a vision of a beautiful watch when holding a handful of scrappy-looking parts. But he had that vision and he now knew that he had it for a reason. If there was anything they were meant to do, it was to transcend their fears and limiting beliefs.

It was time to find out if that was the purpose others could get behind.

Chapter 4 – The Step

Martin managed to convince other parts to hear him out:

"I know none of you here believe in me. No, no, that's not a bad thing." He quickly tried to lighten the mood after he read the deep apologetic sadness on Mrs. Dila's face.

"You were right to not believe in me because I was not committed to **you**. All I cared about was selling you my vision.

"I have been a slave to the *picture*, an addict to the *feeling* that this image gave me. I didn't look at you as a team, I looked at you as an *obstacle to overcome*, figures to play or manipulate, in a way. It was never a conscious thought and I had no bad intentions. Nevertheless, all I cared about was figuring out how to GET ALL OF YOU to play along, so that *I* can get what *I* want!

"For all this, I am deeply sorry. None of this was my intention, but I understand that enlisting ignorance into my team to justify myself won't do much good to any of us either.

"I was astonished to realize all this, and then I was freed from my jail, the jail of the *future*. The jail of 'it's me against the world.' The confinement of awaiting the execution of time and eventually turning into a story told once and forever forgotten."

"Okay, finally you've sobered up and realized that we weren't created to make watches," said a voice from the crowd.

"Yes, we definitely were not created to make watches. But I still believe that we were created to be a part of the watch and I still believe that we have what it takes to do this.

"But this time I will be honest with you – our only chance of succeeding is being open and vulnerable with each other. Our strength is in unity and pooling all of our resources and knowledge together. Only then we can evaluate whether we have what it takes.

"So, all I am asking you is this: If you are so certain that we are nothing but useless scrap, why not take just one step to see if there is something more to this life than waiting for someone to decide our destiny?"

"I am not one to turn down a challenge" Jose spoke up in support of Martin.

"Yeah, what do we have to lose, after all? It is no worse than playing dominoes as we have been doing" supported Mrs. Dila.

Chapter 5 - Where do we begin?

Something in the air had changed. With nothing to prove and nothing to fear, the concept of time itself seemed to have vanished. There was something new, a kind of innocent child-like anticipation as if everyone was waiting to hear the rules of an exciting game they were about to play.

"All right, honorable members of the 'pity basket,' let's start the fun!" started Martin, supported by immediate applause and exclamations from the audience.

"Tell us what to do!" said someone.

"Yeah!" supported others.

"I don't know what to do!" said Martin, in the same cheerful manner.

The crowd was perplexed, and suddenly dead silence consumed the room, interrupted only by bits and pieces of short whispers, of which one could only make out the tone of disappointment.

"Didn't we all agree that I am not the 'know it all' here? Didn't we agree that we are a team and we will act like one? Guys, ignorance is a starting point of any endeavor. Do you know what differentiates stupidity from ignorance? Stupidity is a *state of mind of denying ignorance* to protect the status of a knowledgeable person. But in our situation here, how far will pretentiousness take us? Is someone competing for a CEO position here?" Chuckles from the crowd finally broke the silence.

"We are in this together and one thing that will benefit us most as a team is honesty. We do not have time to waste by beating around the bush. We have a joint mission: to strive as a team, valuing all resources we have and enjoying the journey of creating something special, not just following someone else's map!" finished Martin.

"What resources do we have?!" asked someone.

"Each other!" exclaimed Martin.

"Oh-oh, we are in deep trouble then…" said someone, starting another round of laughter.

"That's right! We are all in trouble, so the only alternative is to get out of it! So…we don't have a manual for building a watch, but we all know something and don't know something about the process. Let's start with the unknowns, by coming up with the biggest list of 'I don't knows' that we can, each of us can contribute with something there is to learn that he or she doesn't know. For example, I don't know what part is put down first, serving as the board for others. I don't know what parts are necessary for the mechanism to work and I don't know whether all of our parts are sufficient and whether all can still perform their job. Let's just lay them all out there, in a single list, and then we see how to deal with each one of these challenges."

Ignorance is a starting point of any endeavor.

Stupidity is a state of mind denying ignorance to protect the status of a knowledgeable person.

One by one, the unknowns were added to the list, just to then be immediately scratched off by someone else who had the answer. It turns out, most unknowns were only unknowns to some, but not to all, so, as a collective, they had a pretty good grip on things!

 The team used Martin's earlier suggestion and mapped out the mechanism of the watch itself, each part's purpose and location relative to others. He was right, everyone knew their neighbors and what their job was!

"We have two crystals…" Martin started

"Hold your horses now," Jose interrupted, "I am in no shape to perform. I have seen enough in my day and I am ready to retire. Besides, my discoloration is not something that goes unnoticed."

"You're right there, the discoloration does make it difficult to see the dial and Fred here is in a lot better shape, forgive my bluntness…" Martin started thinking aloud.

"Well..." Mrs. Dila stepped in. "We are missing a back cover. And…" she paused, "it would take a real soldier to do someone else's job for the good of the team…" She looked at Jose with a kind suggestive expression.

"I don't know..." A ghost of a blush ran across Jose's face. He had been taken off guard by her suggestion. "I've never done this…I don't know if I'll fit. You know, at my age, it's not as easy to adjust to a new job..."

"I think this function will fit your character really well, dear. Out of the spotlight, yet holding everything in place. That pretty much sums up who you are, Jose!" continued Mrs. Dila. Jose's facial expression started revealing subtle signs of agreement, maybe even a little excitement about a new and unexpected career change.

And so, they got to work. In no time, the parts assembled into a very unique watch with a glass back cover that showcased the beautiful mechanism.

Martin was mesmerized, looking at the beautiful creation, when his thoughts were suddenly interrupted by Julie's voice:

"Guys…we have a problem. My arrows won't move," she sounded almost apologetic. "There must be something in the mechanism that doesn't function properly."

"Can that have something to do with the fact that I still see Martin…*outside* the watch!?" Mrs. Dila panicked.

"Looks like we have a loose screw." Martin attempted a joke…unsuccessfully. The silence was unshakable, as everyone tried to understand what had gone wrong.

"Martin! What happened? Where is your place and how did everything fit together without you?! How is it that nobody noticed a missing part?"

"The thing is…" started Martin hesitantly, "I don't know where I was supposed to be. I somehow just assumed there will be a spot for me like there was for the smaller screws…I don't know what happened."

"Well, what was your last position? Where were you stationed?" started investigating Jose.

"I….I can't remember…" stuttered Martin. "I don't remember myself before life in this shelf. I just assumed…" he continued, utterly confused.

"Are you even a watch part?!" someone interrupted with an almost rude impatience.

"I don't know!" Martin said, somewhat irritated "I don't know what my 'label' said about my *intended purpose*. But I tell you this: this watch is exactly what I 'saw,' and this is exactly what I knew my purpose to be… to see this through.

"Of course, I didn't know that I will be seeing it quite literally, from the outside." He chuckled

"You must be so disappointed.." said Mrs Dila with deep sorrow in her voice,

"I am, I won't deny that. But mostly I am deeply surprised. Maybe I am delusional after all because even now that I clearly see that I am not a watch part, I still somehow feel I was destined to be a part of this watch.

"Maybe not knowing about my limitations, allowed me to transcend that. It allowed me to become a part of something in which I had no part by 'design.' Should I have known who I was not, should I have known my vision to be only a dream, I would not have dared to take a leap of faith. Instead, by virtue of blissful ignorance, who I was not, did not define who I was to become! I wouldn't change it for the world, as I am now a part of this watch, even though I remain a non-watch part! I was bestowed freedom from being limited by what I could and couldn't be. I am choosing to see it as a blessing and an honor"

"I don't know what my 'label' said about my intended purpose, but not knowing about my limitations allowed me to transcend that, to become a part of something in which I had no part by 'design.'

*By virtue of blissful ignorance, who I was **not**, did not define who I **was to become!***

Chapter 6 – Fate

The front door opened. Old Larry came in, walking much slower than before, but each step still retained a barely noticeable bounce. The bounce that all those years, day after day, testified to his eagerness to get to his work desk, his creative paradise. He wanted to come in early before the prospective buyer and Tony showed up. He wanted to enjoy the quiet space once again, as he did for so many years in the past. He sat at the desk, unrolling the cloth with his 'specialty watches.'

"Hmmm…what's this? I don't remember leaving a watch here.." He noticed a watch on the edge of the desk. "I guess the kids were right, I might be too old to be on my own, I don't even remember making this!!?" He started looking at the watch, noticing the discolored back cover. "Luis would have been happy to know that what was left of his loyal watch was still serving." He took a moment to reminisce about his friendship with the Marine General who had passed away some years ago.

"Why is it not working? And where is a crown?" Larry started looking for a crown to wind the watch, but it didn't look like he had one on hand. "Ah, hell with it, let's make one! This is the last time I am doing this, no harm in going a little crazy. At my age, it's almost expected!" Larry turned on his old vinyl record and started looking for tools to make a crown...

After an hour of what looked like a mad science experiment, Larry turned off the lamp and pushed back in his chair to admire the work he had done. He turned the crown, winding the watch, once and then twice. Immersed in thought, he kept winding. If he only knew how much hope was concentrated in his hands. Tik, tok, tik, tok…

The door opened and the wind from the outside blew the tiny particles of metal from the desk into the air, and they sparkled, caught in the ray of light as if it was magic dust. The next moment, the room filled with chatter as Evan and Tony walked in.

Larry put the watch down along with the others, to greet his guests.

"See guys," whispered Martin, "sometimes not knowing who you are **not**, allows you to become someone you were always meant to be, against all odds."

*"Sometimes not knowing who you are **not**, allows you to become someone you were always meant to be, against all odds."*

Evan looked at Larry's creations as they kept talking. "I like things with a story, you know. Generic things are available to everyone, but they do not 'speak.' I like things that…like this one for example." He picked up the 'pity basket' watch, "look at it…"

Evan turned it around. "Look at this unlikely back cover, fogging over part of the mechanism as though it is preserving a secret…and the unique crown. It just looks like this watch has a hell of a story to tell! That's what I like!"

Afterword

Hey you! I'm so excited to have shared my story with you!

If you liked it, please help me spread the word by recommending this book to friends and family and (very important!) leaving a review on Amazon, Barnes & Noble, etc.

Our journey doesn't end here, follow me on Instagram: @screwleadership

XOXOXO